Princess Solei Learns of that First Christmas Day

Dr. Shangri-La Durham-Thompson
Illustrated by Vladimir Medina Cebu, LL.B.

Dedication & Acknowledgements

To my granddaughter, Princess Nina Solei; the love of my life and a gift to the world.

Thank you to my wonderfully-accomplished publisher and former English student, Mrs. Letitia Francis-Washington.

Our journey begins.

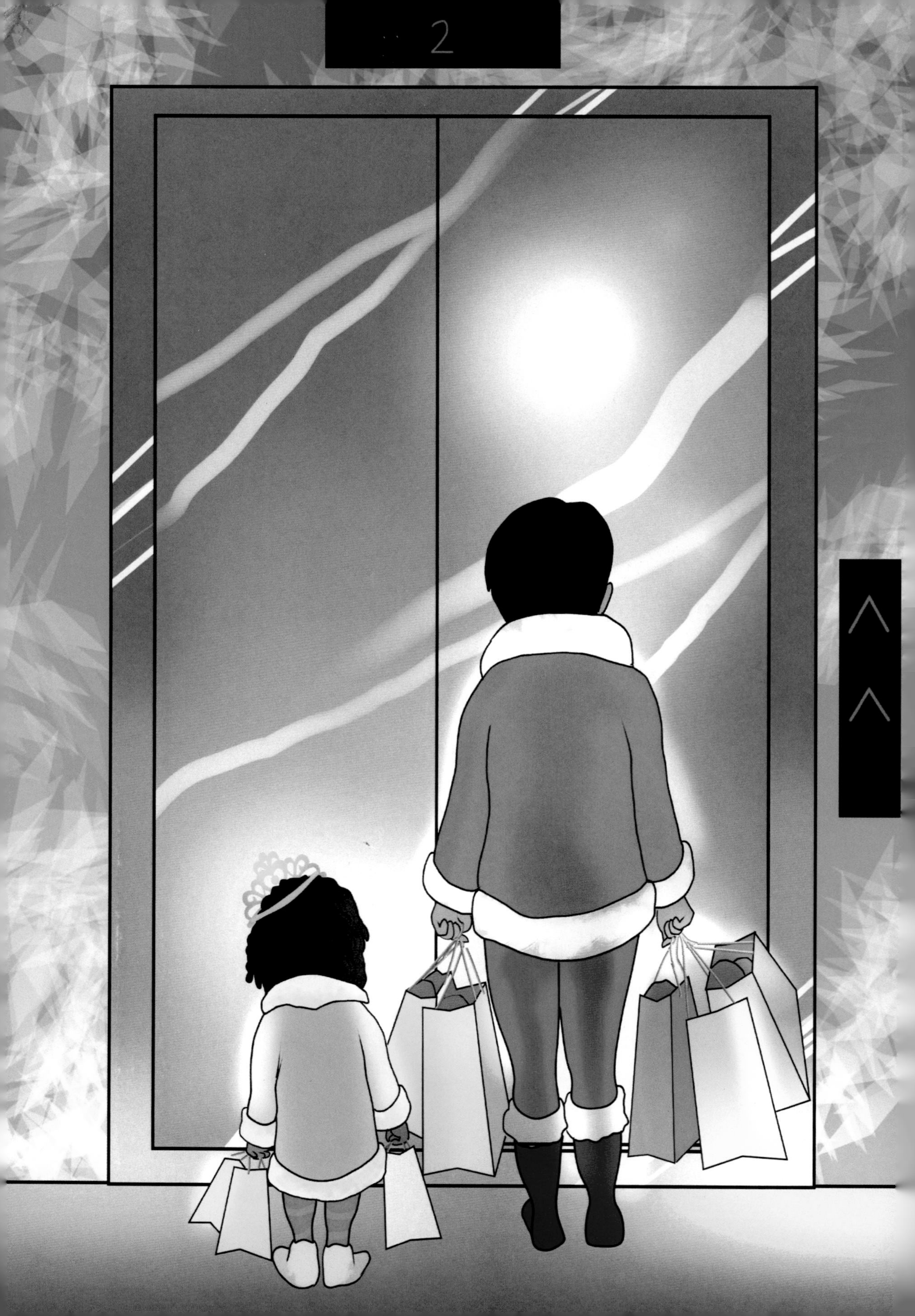
2

I was so excited, I could hardly breath. I pushed the elevator button to the fourth floor about ten times and tried to hold the packages my mom finally agreed I could carry.

"Just be patient, Nina. The elevator will come in a minute," my mom said.

"We must have the slowest elevator in Philadelphia," I muttered.

After what seemed like a year the door opened and I rushed in and almost, but not quite, dropped a package.

"Be careful Nina, and slow down!" my mom said tiredly.

Coincidentally, as I turned the corner (I just learned that word in school. It means just by chance), I saw my friend about to enter her apartment and I called out, excitedly. "Look, Yuna. Look what I found for our trees!" As I tried to pull the unicorn from the bag, another package began to slip.

"Nina," my mom exclaimed, "be careful."

"We just came from the Christmas tree farm. You weren't home when I came to see if you could go with us."

At that moment, Yuna's mom poked her head through the door. I called her Mrs. A. because I couldn't pronounce her name.

"Mrs. A., can Yuna come over and help us decorate our tree? My dad's bringing it up now." I turned to Yuna. "Do you have yours yet? Is it decorated? We can decorate ours tonight. Is yours decorated yet?"

"Goodness Nina, give her a chance to answer one question at a time," mom said.

But Yuna didn't answer. In fact, it looked like she was going to cry.

Suddenly, I knew something was wrong.

Yuna never cries. In fact, my mom said Yuna was easygoing and never superficial.

I wasn't sure what *superficial* meant exactly, but I knew my mom thought Yuna was an angel, and always had a calm spirit. I once giggled with her about switching chocolate chips and putting raisins in her mom's cookie dough, but I knew Yuna would never do that. She was just too sweet. Seeing her look so sad now made me feel bad.

"Is everything alright?" my mom asked Yuna's mom.

"Everything fine," Yuna's mom replied.

Yuna gulped, took a deep breath and wiped her hand across her eyes.

"Yuna, are you crying?" I asked, which was really a dumb question.

"No," she said as she turned away. Now, she looked even more upset, but I could not understand why.

After all, I had just gotten her a unicorn for her tree.

I felt terrible. I had planned for us to have such fun tonight.

My dad agreed to get pizza and we were going to decorate the tree, even though he grumbled that we didn't need one since we were going to Bermuda in a few days.

"Yuna, what's wrong?" I asked again, almost afraid.

"Princess Solei always get everything she wants, and I won't even have tree this year," she said.

"What do you mean?" I asked quietly.

"Princesses always get everything," Yuna said, pointing to me. "Everything!"

I heard her mom gasp.

"Yuna," her mom said. "That's not a nice thing to say to Nina."

Just then, my dad turned the corner dragging the Christmas tree. "A lot of help you guys are," he laughed.

When no one responded, he asked, "What's up?"

Yuna's mom smiled sadly, then gently guided Yuna into their apartment and closed the door

Mom saw that I was about to cry and said, "Everything will be alright Nina. Go with your dad. I'll be there in a minute." She knocked on Yuna's door and Dad nodded that I should go into our apartment.

It was hard to believe that I'd had so much fun this afternoon, even though Yuna didn't go with us, and even though it started to drizzle. We walked through rows and rows of Christmas trees to pick the one I wanted.

Afterwards, we went into the Christmas shop where I'd spotted the unicorn.

Dad had said we didn't need any more ornaments for our tree, but Mom persuaded him to let me have it. After all, she said, it was only one small unicorn.

Then, I'd thought of Yuna and decided to get one for her; after all, she was always bringing stuff for me when she returned from Korea.
Dad looked at the price, sighed and said, "Go ahead Nina, but don't ask for anything else."

We then got hot apple cider and my Dad's favorite...chilly hot dogs.

I was in such a hurry to get home that I didn't want to go to the play area when mom mentioned it. Besides, I told Mom, "It's drizzling."

She knew I wanted to hurry home to show Yuna the unicorns.

On our birthdays, we'd both had unicorn decorations and my Nana had given me a huge one that sat on the special table with all my presents.

Yuna said that my unicorn was the 'specialist' one of all because I was the real princess. Now, her words, that I was a real princess, made me feel, well... not so good.

I must tell you that my Poppie named me Princess Solei and my Nana even wrote a book about me called, *"Presenting Princess Solei on her First Birthday."*

Solei rhymes with day, just so you know.

We went to Toronto to launch the book at the Word on the Street Book Festival. My GiGi went too, and when my aunts, Shelby and Donna got tired of pushing GiGi in her wheelchair, my Poppie pushed her. Even my cousin Kenya went, but my Dad had to work. He said he wished he could have gone, especially when I told him about our visit to Niagara Falls. He's never been there.

Yuna has never been to Bermuda and I have never been to Korea. Maybe one day I'll go with her.

My mom said Korea is a long way away, so I thought that she could come with me to Bermuda.

I wished she could have come *this* Christmas.

Christmas in Bermuda last year was sooo much fun.

I got a zillion presents, even a pink car with a radio and a place to plug in my iPhone.

I showed Yuna a picture of the Gombey's. They danced in the streets when I visited my uncle TJ's friend Sinea's house in St George's last year.

A lot of people follow Gombey's on Boxing day.

That's the day after Christmas.

My Dad used to be a Gombey.

I showed Yuna how he taught me to dance and she laughed and laughed.

My Dad used to dance for the tourists at the Southampton Princess, a big, big hotel in Bermuda.

When the Gombey's dance, people throw them money.

I admitted to Yuna that I was a little afraid of the Gombey's. The drums scared me and so I watched them from Sinea's porch as a big crowd of people walked down the street.

One even carried a whip.

My Dad has his head piece in our living room and my Nana gave me a Gombey doll for Christmas because she said it's a part of my *heritage.*

I don't exactly know what that means, but it must be important.

I was disappointed that Yuna couldn't come to Bermuda since it is a short trip, compared to an airplane ride to Korea. Now, I was even more upset thinking about Yuna not having a Christmas tree. I thought about how she said I was a real princess and that I got everything I wanted. No matter how hard I tried, I couldn't sleep.

I got out of bed and was on my way to the living room where Dad was taking the lights out of boxes when I heard him ask my Mom, "So, what's wrong with Yuna?"

Because I wanted to hear his answer and I was afraid he might stop talking, I stood still. Mom said eavesdropping is wrong, but my feet couldn't move.

"Well, they're going to Korea this year for a few weeks and they just don't want to spend money on a Christmas tree. Yuna's been asking for a pink Cadillac like Nina's for Christmas, and so she's really upset that she won't get a Cadillac or a Christmas tree."

"She and Nina have too much stuff," said Dad. "I don't know why we spend so much at Christmas. Nina doesn't need another toy."

"Says the guy who got everything for Christmas – in expensive Bermuda," said Mom.

"Well, Philly's expensive too, and we agreed that we'd save for that house."

"I know," Mom said, "but I love to give Nina gifts and see her eyes light up."

"I'll bet my parents have bought her a bunch of stuff," Dad said. "My mom needs to follow her own advice."

"What advice?" asked mom.

"Do you remember that poem she wrote about Christmas?"
"Kind of. Is it in her book, '*Battle for Freedom*'? The book's right there on the bookshelf."

Dad got up from the couch, got the book, sat, and turned the pages until he found the poem.

"Listen to this," he said, and he began to read softly:

Only five shopping days till Christmas
To find those perfect gifts
Newspaper ads do justice
And all is well at Smith's.

"What's Smith's?" my Mom asked.

"A store that went out of business eventually, but in its heyday, everyone, including tourists, shopped there. They sold everything and the items were of good quality."

Dad continued reading:

Decorations in place since November
Grocery bills are high
The airline business is booming
Everyone loves waving goodbye
Children have written their Christmas lists
They've been promised the GI Joe.

"What's a GI Joe?" I asked.

"I thought you were asleep Princess," Dad said.
"She should be," Mom stated.

"Maybe she should hear this poem. Come and
sit by me, Princess." Dad patted the space beside
him. "Now where did I leave off?"

Good money will be spent to purchase toy guns

And we'll reap just what we sow

And in all the hustle and bustle

And in all the hurry and rush

And with all the celebrating

And with all the endless fuss

Who will take the time this season

To reflect and to recall
Who will take the time this

The Greatest story ever written.

My Dad paused.

"What's the greatest story ever written?" I asked.

"It's the story of how our Lord came to earth." Dad looked at my mom and shook his head. "You see Ny?" he asked.

My mom's name is *Nyshawana*, but my Dad always calls her *Ny*.

"In all the hustle and bustle, and in all the hurry and rush and with all the celebrating and with all the endless fuss. Who will take the time to remember why we celebrate at all?"

"Princess," my Dad asked, "do you understand what Christmas is really all about?"
"Yes," I replied softly. "Christmas is about getting and giving gifts, like the unicorn I got for Yuna."
"See," said Mom. "At lease she didn't say *Santa*..."
"I didn't forget Santa, Mom. He's going to bring me a lot of presents!" I said.
Dad looked down at the poem. "Let's read this together. Maybe this is the right time for us to remember, and you to learn the *real* meaning of Christmas. Here's what my mom wrote."

I propose that we emphasize this year

The significance of his birth

So, on the 24th of December

Before the children go to bed
Let's gather together young and old alike

For the best story ever read And with hot chocolate beside us

And music playing low
Here's the story to tell our families

Of the savior we love and know...

I clapped my hands. "Mom, Dad stop. Let's get some hot chocolate!"

"It's way past your bedtime, young lady," Mom said.

"There's no school tomorrow," said my Dad. "Let her stay up a few more minutes and we can read the poem together. Ny, will you make us some hot chocolate?" "How about we make hot chocolate together too," my Mom asked and went into the kitchen to boil the water.

Dad had me pass him some lights until the water was hot, then we made the hot cocoa and returned to the living room.

Dad picked up the book. "Okay," he said. "Let's continue reading."

God sent the angel Gabriel from heaven to earth to bring

The news to a young girl named Mary

That she would bear a king

Now, Mary was espoused to Joseph

Engaged to marry, yes that's true

But when she heard the angel's news

She perhaps wondered what Joseph would do

For the angel informed her that she would conceive

Have a baby ... Emmanuel

And that her cousin Elizabeth

Would bear a son as well.

"Do you understand what I've read so far Nina?" Dad asked.
"Not everything," I replied. "I know that Mary had a baby. She was Jesus's mother.

Mom said, "The poem's a little much for a five-year-old."

"Maybe," Dad said, "but we'll read it over and over every Christmas and she'll soon understand the true meaning of the season."

"I'm going to be a writer like Nana when I grow up," I said.

"You can be whatever you want sweetheart," Mom said. "Even a Princess," Dad stated.

"Okay, finish the poem Shan-on, so Nina can go to bed."

"Take your time, *Shan-on*," I said
"What have I told you about calling your father, Shan-on, Nina?"

"Well, that's his name," I replied. "Oops, sorry," I remarked.

"Your mouth is going to cause some problems, I can see," said Dad laughing. "Now let me finish this poem and no more interruptions. We have church tomorrow."

He continued to read.

Now, Elizabeth was barren

She couldn't have kids

But Mary was a virgin girl

But with God, nothing's impossible

For he planned and made this world

And truer words were never spoken

For just as the angel had said

A son was born to Mary

As she lay on a manger bed

For there was no room in the inn that night

When our Lord Jesus was born

But it didn't matter, not his humble birth

Nor the hay that about him adorned.

I raised my hand slowly and dad started to laugh.

"Okay, one last question," he said.

"What does *humble* mean?"

"That's a good question Nina," Mom said. "It means not to place all your attention on what you have."

"You see, Jesus was born in a stable, not a fancy hotel," my Dad said.

"Okay Shan-on, let me finish reading or we'll be here all night," Mom said.

Dad gave her the book and pulled me into his arms.

My mom loves to read.

Can you imagine how the animals must have felt

To be present at that time?

Why I expect they made animal noises

To herald that all was fine

And in the fields as shepherds watched their
flocks by night

There occurred the strangest thing!

A light so bright, as an angel emerged

And to them he too did bring

Good tidings of great joy

And informed them of the birth

Telling them where to find the child

God's son ... born here ... on EARTH

Justifiably, the shepherds were sore afraid

When the angel did first appear

Tending the sheep was a job they knew

But a light? In the fields! brought fear

And as they absorbed the angel's news

There appeared a heavenly host

Praising God in the highest

Father, son and Holy Ghost!

Then one to another, the shepherds they said

"Let us see this which is come to pass"

And they went to Bethlehem – the city of David

To see the babe ... who's arrived ... at last!

For Mica, a prophet had prophesied

That Bethlehem would be

The place where the king from Abraham's seed

Would be born

That was the decree.

Now, the Israelites were under Herod's rule

And when he heard the news, he went wild

For he wanted to be the only king

And planned to kill the child

Thus, he sent for the wise men

Who were seeking to find God's son

Pretending he wanted to pay homage

"What's *homage*?" I asked before I remembered that I wasn't supposed to ask any more questions.

"Well, homage is special honor or respect shown to people publicly. Like a tribute," Dad said.

Before I could open my mouth to ask the next question, he put his finger to my lips and said, "I know, I know. Now you're going to ask me what's a *tribute*. Nina, you're always so full of questions, but if you don't let your mom finish this story, she's going to send you off to bed."

"That's so right," Mom said. "So, where was I?"

And she continued.

Thus, he sent for the wise men

Who were seeking to find God's son

Pretending he wanted to pay homage

But that's not what he'd have done

When they heard the king, they departed,

With gifts of Gold, frankincense and myrrh

But by the time they found the child

He was almost two we concur

And Heron was furious when they failed to return

'For they went home another way

They'd been warned in a dream

That they should not return

And the information to King Herod relay.

Herod in his fury ordered all young boys

Two years and under in age

To be massacred... killed if near Bethlehem found

He was in such an abnormal rage

But God sent an angel to Joseph,

With instructions for all concerned

To go to Egypt and stay until Herod's death

And toNazareth they could return

So, a decree from Caesar Augustus

That all the world should be taxed

Helped to fulfill the prophecy

And allows us now to reflect

On Christmas as a time of giving

So, tell this story on Christmas eve

The gifts symbolize the giving

But it's not just what is received

The wise men gave of their three gifts

But God gave his only son

Who was sent to earth

One of humble birth

To ensure that to God we can come.

"You read that well Ny," Dad said.

Mom leaned over and kissed him.

"Yuck!" I said, and they laughed.

"So," asked Dad, "what did you understand from the poem?"

I raised my hand again.

Mom laughed saying, "You're not in school Nina."

"I know", I giggled. "Well, I got that Jesus was born in a stable where there were animals and that someone wanted to kill him."

Dad looked at Mom. "She got all that? Wow."

"Well, in church they said that Jesus was born in a manger with hay, so I guess that's the stable. And the animals were there, and a king wanted baby Jesus killed, but I don't know why."

"Well," Mom said, "let's just say that the story is about how God loves us so much that He sent Jesus to be born in a manger. Jesus is God's gift to the whole world, and that's why we celebrate Christmas."

"So, Christmas is about accepting that gift. The gift of God's son. I think at one time it was called *Christ Mass*. Meaning *Mass of Christ* and it was shortened to Christmas. So, Christmas is about celebrating the birth of Christ. God loved us so much that He sent his son to live with us and teach us about love. So it really isn't about all the presents you get," Dad said as he tickled me. "Although they're given with love."

"So we should be humble and think of Jesus during this time," Mom whispered, "not about ourselves."

"Can we tell this story to Yuna?" I asked.

"I don't see why not," Mom said. "Although she's Korean, I believe they celebrate Christmas somewhat like we do."

"Maybe she won't be so sad that she doesn't have a tree if she understands that Christmas is about remembering Jesus and His love. But since she may not know, can we give her *our* tree when we leave?"

"How about we put our tree in the foyer for everyone to enjoy?" Mom said. "Trust me, when Yuna gets to Korea and sees all her family, she'll be happy and won't worry about a tree."

"What will I do with the unicorns?" I asked.

Mom looked at my Dad. "Well, reading your Mom's poem tonight seems to be making a difference."

"I want Nana to read the poem again when we get to Bermuda," I said.

"I'm sure she'll be happy to," Mom said.

"I want her to read it with everyone there: Poppie, Uncle TJ, you, me, GiGi, all my cousins, and aunties – Aunt Shelby, Aunt Donna, Aunt Paula, Aunt Hilda, Aunt Valerie, Aunt Jeanmarie, Aunt Brenda, Uncle Bummy, Uncle Danny, God pa Coolie, Uncle Cal, Uncle Danny, Uncle Mac …"

"You already said Uncle Danny. What about Uncle Roddy?" Mom laughed.

"Do you have to encourage this Ny?" my Dad asked. "At this hour?"

"Oh yeah, I almost forgot: Aunt Sharlene, Aunt Mitzy , Aunt Marshie and – "

"Okay, okay," Dad said laughing.

"And we can all have hot chocolate and music playing low," I said.

"The night before Christmas, everyone wants to be in their own home getting ready sweetheart," Dad said.

"But Nana said to gather young and old, alike."

"I think she meant those that live in that particular house," Mom said.

"But we'll be at Nana and Poppie's house, and since Uncle TJ just lives downstairs, can he have hot chocolate with us?" I asked.

"I don't think you could keep your Uncle TJ away," Dad said.

"So, let me count. There will be you, Mama, Nana, Poppie and Uncle TJ and ME!" I exclaimed. "Can we read the poem again, Mom? It's not too late. I won't ask any questions this time. I promise, I'll just listen."

"Nina," my Mom said. "How about you let Nana read it when we get to Bermuda? Now off to bed you go."

"Can you teach me how to read all the big words before we go to Bermuda?" I asked. "I'll practice so that I can read it to Nana, and maybe next year I can read it in church. I'll be able to read all the big words, like *humble*."

"Maybe you can memorize the first part of the poem and recite it for your Nana. She'd love that," Mom said and she looked at dad. "That should give us some peace."

"What does *recite* mean?" I asked.

"Yet another question Princess Solei. Recite means to say the words from memory, like you did for your poem at school," Dad answered.

"I can do that," I said. "I have a great memory."

"She takes after me," my Dad said. "Admit it... come on, pay *homage*, Ny."

"Yeah," said Mom. "Such *humility*."

About The Author

Dr. Shangri-La Durham-Thompson, an educator of over forty years, a past school principal and a church school superintendent appreciates the importance of the written and spoken word especially in the lives of children. Today, she is the grandmother to Princess Solei (so named by her Poppie). After reading to her grandbaby, Dr. Durham-Thompson decided to write a book as her gift to Nina for her birthday. That first book, *Presenting Princess Solei on Her First Birthday*

Made in the USA
Columbia, SC
22 November 2022